Dear Parent:
Your child's love of reading starts here!

Every child learns to read in a different way and at his or her own speed. Some go back and forth between reading levels and read favorite books again and again. Others read through each level in order. You can help your young reader improve and become more confident by encouraging his or her own interests and abilities. From books your child reads with you to the first books he or she reads alone, there are I Can Read Books for every stage of reading:

SHARED READING
Basic language, word repetition, and whimsical illustrations, ideal for sharing with your emergent reader

BEGINNING READING
Short sentences, familiar words, and simple concepts for children eager to read on their own

READING WITH HELP
Engaging stories, longer sentences, and language play for developing readers

READING ALONE
Complex plots, challenging vocabulary, and high-interest topics for the independent reader

ADVANCED READING
Short paragraphs, chapters, and exciting themes for the perfect bridge to chapter books

I Can Read Books have introduced children to the joy of reading since 1957. Featuring award-winning authors and illustrators and a fabulous cast of beloved characters, I Can Read Books set the standard for beginning readers.

A lifetime of discovery begins with the magical words "I Can Read!"

Visit www.icanread.com for information
on enriching your child's reading experience.

Fancy NANCY Story Collection

I Can Read!

5 EARLY READERS

Fancy NANCY Story Collection

by Jane O'Connor
pictures based on
the art of Robin Preiss Glasser

HARPER
An Imprint of HarperCollinsPublishers

Table of Contents

Fancy NANCY and the Boy from Paris

by Jane O'Connor

cover illustration by Robin Preiss Glasser

interior illustrations by Ted Enik

I almost always get to school early.

But on Monday I am tardy.

(That's a fancy word for late.)

I come in and see a new kid.

He is standing next to Ms. Glass.

"Robert comes from Paris!"

Ms. Glass is telling everyone.

"He just moved here."

Paris!

Paris is a city in France.

It is gorgeous.

(That is a fancy word for beautiful.)

13

"Bonjour," I say in the book nook.

(In French that means "hello.")

"I am Nancy.

I never met anybody

from Paris before."

I speak slowly so he will understand.

"It's really nice there," Robert says.

"I miss it."

He has a book on cowboys.

He probably wants to learn

all about this country.

"I want to go there someday."

I show him my book.

It is about a dog in Paris.

"Do you like the United States?"

"Yes," says Robert. "Don't you?"

"Yes, I do," I say.

"I've lived here all my life."

Then Ms. Glass puts a finger
to her mouth.

"This is not talking time," she says.

"This is reading time."

On Tuesday

I sit next to Robert at lunch.

"Have you ever been

to the Eiffel Tower?"

I ask him.

Robert nods and swallows.

"Lots of times.

Our house was near it."

I tell Robert,

"I know about the Eiffel Tower.

There's a poster of it in my room.

I know lots about Paris."

I share some of my lunch.

"These are donut holes," I say.

Robert gives me a funny look.

"I know that.

I have eaten donut holes before."

That night

I tell my mom and dad about Robert.

"He is very nice.

He already speaks English.

I want to be his friend.

How do you say friend in French?"

"The word is *ami*," my mom says.

"You say it like this: ah-mee."

I love French.

Everything sounds so fancy!

"Why don't you ask him

over to play?" my dad says.

So the next day I do.

"We can play soccer.

Did you play soccer in Paris?"

"Sure. All the time," Robert says.

"I am a good kicker.

I can come on Friday."

On Thursday it is Show and Share.

Robert brings in a toy horse.

It is brown and white.

"My grandpa has a horse like this."

Then Robert passes around a photo.

"I miss her a lot.

Her name is Belle.

In French that means beautiful."

"Belle," I say to myself.

Now I know another French word.

On Friday Mom is at work.

Mrs. DeVine picks us up from school.

"Mrs. DeVine lives next door,"

I tell Robert.

"Robert is from Paris,"

I tell Mrs. DeVine.

At home

we make a tent in the yard.

We pretend bears are outside.

We pretend to be terrified.

(That's a fancy word for scared.)

Then we play soccer.

We let my little sister play too.

Robert is a great kicker.

My dog runs around the yard.

"That's Frenchy," I tell Robert.

"She is not really French.

But you will like her anyway."

We go inside and

I show Robert my room.

"See? There's the Eiffel Tower,"

I say.

"Yes," says Robert.

"But that one does not
have a cowboy hat on it.
That Eiffel Tower is in Paris, France.
It is taller, and it is more famous.
But we have an Eiffel Tower too.
Our Eiffel Tower has a cowboy hat
on the top."

Wait a minute! I am very perplexed.

(That's a fancy word for mixed up.)

"But you're from Paris, France," I say.

"Aren't you?"

"No, I am from Texas.

Paris, Texas," Robert says.

"Ms. Glass told everybody

that the first day."

Robert shows me Paris, Texas,

on my globe.

Oh!

I guess I missed that part.

And I feel a little silly.

But not for long.

After all,

I have a new *ami*,

even if he isn't French.

Fancy Nancy's Fancy Words

These are the fancy words in this book:

Ami—"friend" in French (you say it like this: ah-mee)

Belle—"beautiful" in French (you say it like this: bell)

Bonjour—"hello" in French (you say it like this: bohn-joor)

Gorgeous—beautiful

Perplexed—mixed up

Tardy—late

Terrified—scared

Fancy NANCY

Splendid Speller

by Jane O'Connor

cover illustration by Robin Preiss Glasser

interior illustrations by Ted Enik

I don't mean to brag,

but I am a splendid speller.

S-P-L-E-N-D-I-D.

(Splendid is even better than great.)

Bree is a splendid speller too.

We practice spelling

in our clubhouse after school.

I can even spell in French!

C-H-I-E-N means "dog."

You say it like this—SHEE-enn.

My sister is very impressed.

(Impressed means

she thinks I'm great.)

My sister cannot spell any words.

My parents spell out stuff

they don't want her to hear.

They used to fool me this way,

but not anymore.

She has to get a shot,

S-H-O-T,

at her checkup tomorrow.

45

At school today, Ms. Glass says,

"Our first spelling test

is on Friday."

Here is the list of test words.

pass   glass

class   happy

sad   glad

mad   peek

week   giggle

We write down the words.

Some kids make faces.

They think the words are hard.

But Bree and I are happy.

H-A-P-P-Y.

This test will be easy!

At dinner I practice some words.

"Please P-A-S-S the carrots.

May I have a G-L-A-S-S of milk?"

Dad claps and says, "Bravo!"

"I don't mean to brag," I say,

"but Bree and I

are the best spellers

in the C-L-A-S-S."

Later I memorize

the harder words.

(Memorize is fancy for

learn by heart.)

The hardest is "giggle."

G-I-G-G-L-E.

It has so many Gs!

I practice all week.

W-E-E-K.

It will be splendid

to spell every word right.

By Friday I am ready.

Ms. Glass says each word slowly.

The last one is "giggle."

I write down G-I-G-L-E.

Is that right?

I am not sure.

I try it another way.

G-I-G-G-L-E.

Is that right?

Then I do something wicked.

(Wicked is way worse than bad.)

I peek, P-E-E-K, at Bree's paper!

Bree has G-I-G-G-L-E.

I bet Bree is right.

I start to fix my word.

I want to get all the words right.

I want to be a splendid speller.

Then I stop.

"No, no, no," I say to myself.

I hand in my test to Ms. Glass.

If she knew I peeked,

I bet she would hate me!

At the playground,

I do not play with any kids.

At lunch,

I do not eat my cookies.

I do not sing in music.

At the end of the day,

we get back our tests.

I got one wrong.

"Giggle."

Miss Glass takes me aside.

"What's wrong, Nancy?" she asks.

"Are you upset about the test?

You did very well."

I tell her what I did.

I cry so hard I get hiccups.

"I am a wicked cheater."

Ms. Glass says,

"Nancy, it was wrong

to peek at Bree's paper.

But you did not cheat.

You stopped before you cheated.

I am proud of you for that."

"You are?" I say.

I still feel sad.

S-A-D.

But I do not feel so wicked.

On the way home,

I confess to Bree.

(Confess means telling

something bad you did.)

She forgives me.

She shows me her test.

"I forgot a *p* in 'happy,'" she says.

Maybe we are not always

splendid spellers,

but we are always splendid friends!

Fancy Nancy's Fancy Words

These are the fancy words in this book:

Chien—"dog" in French (you say it like this: SHEE-enn)

Confess—telling someone something bad that you did

Impressed—thinking someone or something is great

Memorize—learn by heart

Splendid—even better than great

Wicked—way worse than bad

by Jane O'Connor

cover illustration by Robin Preiss Glasser

interior illustrations by Ted Enik

Bree can't come over

after school today.

She is going to an eye doctor.

In school, her eyes hurt a lot.

It is very distressing.

(That's like upsetting—only fancier.)

I hope the eye doctor helps her.

That night,

Bree sends a note in our basket.

"I have a surprise," the note says.

I send back a note.

"Tell me! Tell me!" it says.

Bree sends another note.

"You have to wait until tomorrow."

I am not very good at waiting.

The next morning,

I race over to Bree's house.

Out she comes.

Bree is wearing glasses!

They are for reading.

Her eyes won't hurt anymore.

"Ooh la la!" I say.

"You look spectacular."

(That's a fancy word for great.)

Bree's glasses are lavender.

That's fancy for light purple.

And they glitter.

Bree puts her glasses

in a silver case.

Her glasses and case

are both so fancy!

At school,

Bree tells our class

about the eye doctor.

Bree had to read a chart

with lots of letters on it.

The letters went from big to tiny.

"Glasses are like magic.

I can read tiny stuff now," she says.

"Nothing looks blurry!"

"Your glasses are most becoming,"

Ms. Glass says.

That's a fancy word

I have never heard before.

Ms. Glass says it means pretty.

"I think Bree looks spectacular!"

I say.

Then Ms. Glass tells us

that spectacles is another word

for eyeglasses.

Wow! Bree has spectacular spectacles.

During math time,

Bree wears her glasses.

In the library,

she wears her glasses.

The eye doctor also gave Bree

a little silk hankie

for cleaning her glasses.

It is pink with purple polka dots.

I wish I had a hankie like that.

I wish I had a silver case.

Most of all,

I wish I had lavender glasses

with glitter.

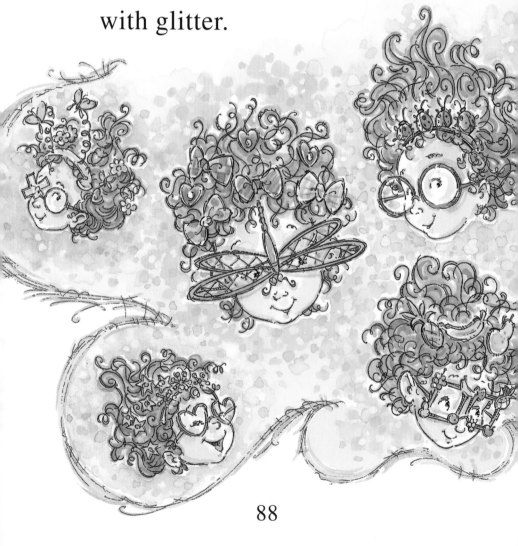

Then I start to wonder.

Maybe I do need glasses.

At dinner,

I am pretty sure

my food looks blurry.

After dinner, I do a puzzle.

It has tiny pieces

and is very challenging.

(That's fancy for hard.)

I try squinting. Yes!

I do think everything

looks clearer now.

Later my mom comes into my room.

I am reading in the dark.

"That is very bad for your eyes!"

Mom says.

"I know," I say.

Then I tell Mom about Bree.

"I bet she'll get a fancy necklace,

like the one Ms. Glass wears.

It's not fair!" I say.

"I want glasses."

My mom does not get mad.

She says Bree has glasses because

her eyes need them.

"Your eyes are fine.

You are a lucky girl."

I know that, but I still want them.

Then I get an idea
that is spectacular.
My mom helps me.

My old sunglasses had only one lens.

So I popped out the other.

My glasses are just pretend.

But don't I look fancy?

Fancy Nancy's Fancy Words

These are the fancy words in this book:

Becoming—pretty

Challenging—hard

Distressing—very upsetting

Lavender—light purple

Spectacles—eyeglasses

Spectacular—great

Fancy NANCY

The Dazzling Book Report

by Jane O'Connor

cover illustration by Robin Preiss Glasser

interior illustrations by Ted Enik

Monday is my favorite day.

Why?

Monday is Library Day.

Before we leave, we select a book.

(Select is a fancy word for pick.)

It is like getting a present

for a week!

Bree selects a book on dinosaurs.

Robert selects a book
of funny poems.

Teddy selects a scary story.

I select a book

about an Indian girl.

She has a fancy name,

Sacajawea.

You say it like this:

SACK-uh-jah-WAY-ah.

Later Ms. Glass has

thrilling news.

(Thrilling is even more exciting

than exciting.)

We get to do a book report!

"Your first book report.

How grown up!"

my mom says at dinner.

"Yes, I know," I say.

"My book is a biography.

It is about a real person."

After dinner I read my book.

Dad helps with the hard words.

I learn all about Sacajawea.

Sacajawea was a princess.

She lived two hundred years ago

out West.

She helped two explorers

reach the Pacific Ocean.

Mom takes me to the art store.

I need stuff for

the cover of my book report.

I want it to be great!

(I am the second-best artist

in our class.

This isn't bragging.

You can ask anybody.)

I get a bag of little beads,

some yarn,

and markers.

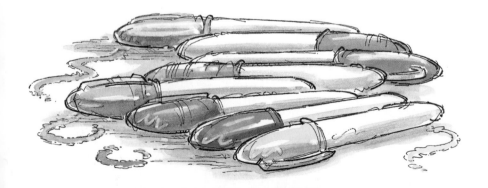

I start working on the cover.

I work on it every night.

I make Sacajawea look very brave,

because she was.

She found food for the explorers.

She kept them safe from enemies.

"Just remember to
leave time for the words,"
Mom keeps saying.
"I will. I will," I tell her.

"Ms. Glass wants you
to write about the book,"
Dad says over and over.
"That's what a report is."
"I know that!" I tell him.
Writing the words will be easy.

Ta-da! The cover is finished.

Sacajawea has yarn braids.

Beads and fringe are glued

on her clothes.

I must admit it is dazzling.

(That is fancy for eye-popping.)

Now I will write my report.

I get out lined paper

and a pen with a plume.

(That's a fancy word for feather.)

The trouble is, I am tired.

I know all about Sacajawea.

But the right words won't come.

What am I going to do?

I have to hand in my report tomorrow!

"I am desperate!" I tell Mom.

(That means I'm in trouble.)

Mom lets me stay up longer.

Still my report ends up

only two sentences long.

The next day,

everyone sees my cover

and says, "Wow!"

But hearing other reports

makes me nervous.

All of them are longer

than mine.

All of them are more interesting.

I read my report.

"Sacajawea was a heroine.

She helped people in trouble."

Everybody waits to hear more.

But there is no more.

I am crestfallen.

(That is fancy for sad and ashamed.)

"I spent too much time

on the cover,"

I tell Ms. Glass.

Ms. Glass understands.

"Why don't you tell the class about your book?"

So I do.

I tell them all about

the brave things Sacajawea did.

Sacajawea was a heroine.

Ms. Glass is a heroine too.

At least, she is to me!

Fancy Nancy's Fancy Words

These are the fancy words in this book:

Biography—a story about a real person

Crestfallen—sad and ashamed

Dazzling—eye-popping, a knockout

Desperate—feeling trapped

Heroine—a girl or a woman who is brave and helps people

Plume—feather

Select—to pick

Thrilling—even more exciting than exciting

Fancy NANCY
Sees Stars

by Jane O'Connor

cover illustration by Robin Preiss Glasser

interior illustrations by Ted Enik

Stars are so fascinating.

(That's a fancy word

for interesting.)

I love how they sparkle in the sky.

Tonight is our class trip.

Yes! It's a class trip at night!

We are going to the planetarium.

That is a museum

about stars and planets.

Ms. Glass tells us,

"The show starts at eight.

We will all meet there."

I smile at my friend Robert.

My parents are taking Robert and me.

Then Ms. Glass asks,

"What star is closest to Earth?"

That's easy.

It's the sun.

"What do you call stars

that make a picture?"

asks Ms. Glass.

Robert and Bree have both forgotten.

"I know, I know," I say.

"A constellation."

Ms. Glass nods.

On the wall are pictures.

There's the hunter and the crab

and the Big Dipper.

It looks like a big spoon.

CANCER
THE
CRAB

ORION
THE
HUNTER

We will see all of them at the show.

I can hardly wait.

At home, Robert and I

put glow-in-the-dark stickers

on our T-shirts.

Mine has the Big Dipper.

Robert has the hunter on his.

We spin my mobile

and watch the planets orbit the sun.

(Orbit is a fancy word.

It means to travel in a circle.)

Then we pretend to orbit

until we get dizzy.

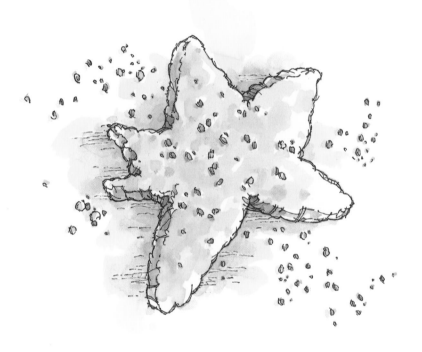

Later, we bake star cookies.

Sprinkles make them sparkle.

"The sun is a star,"

I tell my sister.

"It is the closest star,

so we see it in the day."

After dinner,

we wait for the baby-sitter.

She is very late.

Dad says not to worry.

We have plenty of time.

At last we get in the car.

Drip, drip, drip.

It is raining.

The rain comes down

harder and harder.

Dad drives slower and slower.

It is getting later and later.

146

A policeman comes over.

"The road is closed,"

he tells my parents.

"There is too much water."

Oh no!

There are cars in front of us.

There are cars behind us.

We are stuck!

"The show is starting soon!"

Robert says.

"We will not make it."

Drip, drip, drip goes the rain.

Drip, drip, drip go my tears.

Robert and I are so sad.

We do not even want any cookies.

At last the cars move

and the rain stops.

But it is too late.

The night sky show is over.

By the time we get home,

the sky is full of stars.

They are brilliant!

(That's a fancy word

for shiny and bright.)

152

I get a brilliant idea.

(Brilliant also means very smart.)

We can have

our own night sky show.

153

My parents get my sister.

We set up beach chairs.

Mom lights candles.

Dad puts the cookies on a tray.

We eat alfresco.

(That's fancy for eating outdoors.)

We watch the stars.

We see the North Star.

We see the Big Dipper.

All at once,

something zooms across the sky.

"A shooting star," Dad says.

"Make a wish!"

I tell Dad it is not a star.

It is a meteor.

But I make a wish anyway.

The next day Ms. Glass says,

"Everyone missed the show

because of the storm.

So we will go next week."

Everybody is very happy.

And guess what? My wish came true!

Fancy Nancy's Fancy Words

These are the fancy words in this book:

Alfresco—outside; eating outside is called eating alfresco

Brilliant—bright and shiny, or very, very smart

Constellation—a group of stars that make a picture

Fascinating—very interesting

Meteor—a piece of a comet that leaves a blazing streak as it travels across the sky (you say it like this: me-tee-or)

Orbit—to circle around something

Planetarium—a museum about stars and planets